Squelch!

First published 2005
Evans Brothers Limited
2A Portman Mansions
Chiltern Street
London WIU 6NR

British Library Cataloguing in Publication Data
Woodward, Kay
      Squelch!. - (Twisters)
      1. Children's stories - Pictorial works
      I. Title
      823.9'2 [J]

ISBN 0 237 52884 3

Printed in China by WKT Company Limited

Series Editor: Nick Turpin
Design: Robert Walster
Production: Jenny Mulvanny
Series Consultant: Gill Matthews

Squelch!

Kay Woodward
and Stefania Colnaghi

Evans

There's mud in
the garden.

Squelch!

8

There's paint on the shelf.

9

Slop!

There's snow on the ground.

Crunch!

"I'm hungry."

"I'll wash my hands."

There's pizza for tea.

S-t-r-e-t-c-h!

There's jam for
the pudding.

Plop!

"You're filthy!
Time for a bath."

26

Splash!

"Now you're nice and clean."

Why not try reading another Twisters book?

Not-so-silly Sausage by Stella Gurney and Liz Million
ISBN 0 237 52875 4
Nick's Birthday by Jane Oliver and Silvia Raga
ISBN 0 237 52896 7
Out Went Sam by Nick Turpin and Barbara Nascimbeni
ISBN 0 237 52894 0
Yummy Scrummy by Paul Harrison and Belinda Worsley
ISBN 0 237 52876 2
Squelch! by Kay Woodward and Stefania Colnaghi
ISBN 0 237 52895 9
Sally Sails the Seas by Stella Gurney and Belinda Worsley
ISBN 0 237 52893 2

If you liked Twisters try a ZigZag!

Dinosaur Planet by David Orme and Fabiano Fiorin
ISBN 0 237 52793 6
Tall Tilly by Jillian Powell and Tim Archbold
ISBN 0 237 52794 4
Batty Betty's Spells by Hilary Robinson and Belinda Worsley
ISBN 0 237 52795 2
The Thirsty Moose by David Orme and Mike Gordon
ISBN 0 237 52792 8
The Clumsy Cow by Julia Moffatt and Lisa Williams
ISBN 0 237 52790 1
Open Wide! by Julia Moffatt and Anni Axworthy
ISBN 0 237 52791 X
Too Small by Kay Woodward and Deborah van de Leijgraaf
ISBN 0 237 52777 4
I Wish I Was An Alien by Vivian French and Lisa Williams
ISBN 0 237 52776 6
The Disappearing Cheese by Paul Harrison and Ruth Rivers
ISBN 0 237 52775 8
Terry the Flying Turtle by Anna Wilson and Mike Gordon
ISBN 0 237 52774 X
Pet To School Day by Hilary Robinson and Tim Archbold
ISBN 0 237 52773 1
The Cat in the Coat by Vivian French and Alison Bartlett
ISBN 0 237 52772 3